Holiday Short Stories

Morbier Impossible

A Second Chance

The Magic of Sharing

The Case of the Disappearing Gingerbread City

The Lucia Crown

Down the Memory Aisle

Down the Memory Aisle

by R.W. Wallace

Copyright © 2021 by R.W. Wallace

Cover by R.W. Wallace

Cover Illustration 2199936 © Kotenko | Depositphotos

All characters and events in this book, other than those clearly in the public domain, are fictitious and any resemblance to real persons, living or dead, is purely coincidental.

All rights reserved. No part of this publication may be reproduced, distributed, or transmitted in any form or by any means, including photocopying, recording, or other electronic or mechanical methods, without the prior written permission of the publisher, except in the case of brief quotations embodied in critical reviews and certain other noncommercial uses permitted by copyright law.

www.rwwallace.com

ISBN ebook: [979-10-95707-84-4]

ISBN paperback: [979-10-95707-83-7]

A Short Holiday Romance

R.W. WALLACE
FROM THE AUTHOR OF FLIRTING IN PLAIN SIGHT

Down the Memory Aisle

Memory's an odd thing. It's like your mind is made up of endless walls of filing cabinets, every file a separate memory. Some are easily accessible, in the main aisles where you walk down every day, the cabinet drawers sliding open easily on well-greased rails, and the sheets filed into sections that you know by heart so you don't even need to look to pull out the right one.

The names of your best friends, right there on the left. The color of your childhood bedroom, up there in the right hand corner. The name of your favorite chocolate cake from the bakery downstairs, down here, close to the floor, filed next to the price of pasta and a romantic date from last year. Don't bother trying to understand. It makes sense to me, that's all that matters.

Some files are always here, on the main aisle, but can't quite decide where their place is. Like the car keys. On the table by the door? In the ignition? In the pants I just threw in the wash? It's one of the three. If I can't remember which one, I'll just open all three cabinets.

It's very rare for a file to completely disappear. If I heard something, said something, lived something, I *will* remember it if someone nudges me in the right direction. *You know, we were in that seafood restaurant in Bergen and it was absolutely pouring outside. A foreigner tried to use an umbrella and it was thrown into the fjord. Remember that dress you were wearing? It was fabulous.* Oh, right. Down the third corridor on the right, I think, then down a flight of stairs and...there! I have to put all my weight into pulling the drawer open, squeaking all the way. But there, in the next-to-last folder, is the fabulous blue dress I wore that night. I spilled red wine down the front just before leaving and could never get it clean. If I had to, I could probably find the file on what I did with the dress, but that's not the point here.

The point is, the mind is vast. And some hallways—hell, entire floors—we don't walk down for years. We know it's there, and it's not a scary place or anything, we just haven't had an excuse to visit. Nobody switched on a light, reminding us of the elevator. Nobody offered to play hide-and-seek in the stacks.

So when you do remember all those memories you stored away, it can be a bit of a shock. Switch on the light and realize it's not just a light bulb dangling from the ceiling, but a sparkling chandelier. The filing cabinets aren't straight rows of boring black like on the main aisle, but a jumble of blue and red and orange, not a one the same size or design as its neighbor, files poking out of hastily closed drawers or lying discarded on the psychedelically carpeted floor.

If you'd thought about it, you'd have known there were several rooms, but you always only glanced at the closest two in passing. The dozens and dozens of rooms farther back never even showed up on your GPS in the past decade.

And now, because of one missed bus, I'm back on that crazy teen-aged carpet. All the lights are on, I remember the alleys in the back and the cozy loveseat around the corner. Or maybe I should say freezing park bench...

I don't come back to Trondheim very often. I grew up here and spent my first eighteen years trudging up and down the hills surrounding the city center. School, soccer, handball, choir, cross country skiing, hanging out with friends. All the usual stuff. I wasn't one of the cool kids, but neither was I one of the uncool ones. More the average girl that nobody really noticed.

Except the one guy who did.

See, that's the revelation that has me literally freezing my ass off on a park bench in the middle of the night two days after Christmas.

I'd forgotten about Magnus. Somehow. When I tell someone about my formative years in Trondheim, he never even comes to mind. I'll talk about my choice of high school and my grades, my naive hopes for the future. I'll mention my group of friends, which has somehow managed to keep in touch for over a decade, despite two of us having moved to a different part of the country. I'll even recount the memorable soccer match where we lost 17-0, the day I admitted to myself I'd never be a great player and should perhaps try out some other sports. Something with less running after a ball.

But I never mention, because I never think of, the boy who made me feel special one night in December my senior year in high school.

We were sitting right here, on this bench, both of us shaking from equal parts laughter and cold, when he kissed me. Said he'd been watching me, that he liked me.

I still have trouble believing it.

I had negotiated for hours with my parents to be allowed to go to the party at my friend Kathrine's place on December 26th. Traditionally, Christmas Eve is celebrated with family. Christmas Mass, Christmas dinner, Christmas gifts, Christmas beer... The salmon is for Christmas Day, and it's still a family affair. Then, after two whole days of family, there's a need for some time off, so on the 26th, it's time to party—with friends.

But alcohol is usually abundant at these parties, even the ones with participants under the legal age of eighteen, and my parents weren't very keen on letting me go. I think the only reason they let me was that I could legally drink, so their arguments were moot. I'd been eighteen for two whole months, and had yet to come home drunk. At some point, they'd have to start trusting me.

They did blindside me a little, though. At the time, I was furious, but as the events of the evening unfolded, they were easily forgiven. Since the party was several kilometers from our house, they didn't want me to be walking around alone at night. So they arranged for a boy who was going to the same party, and just happened to be the son of one of my dad's colleagues, to accompany me.

They got me a babysitter.

I was still screaming my head off at my mother when he knocked on our door. Feeling more attached to my reputation (or lack thereof) than to putting my mother in her place, I stopped complaining and promised my parents there would be *words* the next day. Took some pleasure in using that expression on them. I opened the front door and found myself face-to-face with an uncertain smile and gentle green eyes.

"You're Emma?" Magnus said. Although he was clearly nervous, there was a self-assurance about him that I liked. Not arrogance, far from it, but he wasn't the type who would fold immediately if he met resistance.

I recognized him. He'd been a year ahead of me, so was probably off studying something or other now. Didn't know much more, though.

A glance at my mother showed she was way too interested for comfort. No way was I giving her anything after the surprise she'd just sprung on me. "Yep, that's me," I said. "Let's go." I grabbed my coat, jumped into my boots, and off we went.

Trondheim center is at sea level, with the fjord on one side and the Nidelva river slinging around to cover the rest. Bakklandet, where our party was held, is a small neighborhood made up of cutesy, colorful, and ancient wooden houses on the north side of the river, squeezed in between the cold river and the hills rising toward where I lived. The slope is quite steep and the bike elevator has been the source of many articles and travel blogs.

That's not the steepest climb, though. That comes at the very top, just before reaching the spot housing the local radio tower on Tyholt. In excellent Norwegian style, someone figured the fastest route from A to B was a straight line, so they made a road go right down from top to bottom. Then they also made a zig-zagging grid of normally sloped roads throughout the hillside, allowing the inhabitants to get in and out without risking life and limbs every time.

I'm sure it won't surprise anybody to learn that nobody below the age of twenty would never consider choosing the zig-zags over the straight line, be it to go up or down, in summer or winter, on foot or by bike. We all have winter tires, after all.

Tonight I'm going up the infamous climb, away from the city center. But back then, on that magical night, we had to go *down* the steep descent. And it was covered in ice. We'd been lucky enough to have a white Christmas on the 24th, then on the 25th, everything started to melt. Only to freeze again on the 26th. So the roads that hadn't been a first priority for the snow plows were covered in a ten centimeter thick layer of iced slush.

We'd stopped at the top to consider our options. At this point, we'd been walking and talking for twenty minutes and were becoming comfortable with each other. Magnus had told me about his first year studying Physics at the university in Oslo and I'd recounted all the ridiculous drama surrounding my friends in school. I was comfortable talking to him and was already looking forward to walking back home with him after the party.

"There's no way we're making it down the slope without falling on our asses at least five times," Magnus said. The ice was so smooth, the moonlight reflected a perfect image up at us.

Laid out below us, Trondheim by night. The cathedral towered over everything else with its stone facade and tall green spire. The old white fort built to defend against attackers coming in the fjord was beautifully lit up at the bottom of the steep incline, halfway down the hill. And the dark expanse of the fjord on the right. Breathing in the crisp December air, I reveled in the magic of it all.

Taking the sensible route down didn't sound very magical. Or fun. It *would* buy me more time alone with Magnus, but I'd need more to step down from the challenge he'd issued.

"Five times?" I scoffed. "How old and scared are you? It's all about confidence. You accept the fact you'll slip and go with it. I say two falls, max, when we slide off the road, and, you know, possibly when we need to slow down." We'd cross the zig-zagging roads several times but the chances of meeting cars were slim to none. On the large road at the bottom, though...

"You're proposing we slide down in one go?" Magnus's smile said he was game, his tone gave away his apprehension.

I couldn't stop grinning. Couldn't remember the last time I'd had so much fun. "There's two of us. If we hold onto each other, we'll have four feet. Should be pretty stable."

"As a student in Physics, I'd like to point out that your logic most likely won't hold up against reality." But he was scoping out the slope below us, picking out the dangerous spots, the greatest challenges.

"Ah!" I held up a gloved finger. "Most likely. Where there's uncertainty, there's hope."

"That's not how the saying goes."

Shrugging, I checked my coat was securely closed, that all my pockets were sealed, that my phone was safely tucked away against my breast. I flashed my best smile and looked straight into his beautiful green eyes. "You scared?"

He couldn't back down now.

Standing at the very edge of the downward slope, we took up wide stances and grabbed each other's elbows. It felt pretty stable.

Until we gave a push and set off down the slope. That ice was *smooth*. We gained speed even faster than when rolling down here on a bike in summer without using the brakes. Which is to mean, *fast*.

We were lucky our aim wasn't better. If we'd managed to stay in the middle of the road, we'd have ended up going fast enough to break something when we inevitably fell. As it were, we only made it to the first zig-zag. By then, we'd gotten turned around at least a dozen times already and my head was spinning. All my energy and focus went into staying on my feet and holding onto Magnus for dear life. When we hit that other road, the gravel we hadn't incorporated into our calculations tripped us up.

I lost my footing but kept hold of Magnus. He emitted a loud *oof* when I landed on his chest and then a grunt when we slid into the ditch.

"Ouch," he groaned. "Told you we wouldn't make it." He chuckled.

I couldn't believe I'd done something so crazy. It was totally unlike me. But it was so much *fun*! I started giggling uncontrollably, which didn't help in the least with catching my breath.

"Can I assume you're not hurt?" Magnus asked. He was lying flat in the ditch, making for a comfortable mattress for me. His back must have been freezing, though.

"I'm fine," I managed. "You didn't break anything? I wonder what my parents would say if I broke the babysitter?"

"As long as I don't get blamed for breaking the baby, everything's fine." He anticipated my slug and held up his arms to protect his face. His whole body vibrated as he laughed.

With a lot of slipping, a couple of accidental knees to Magnus's midsection, and a fair amount of swearing, we made it out of the ditch and onto the grassy patch on the side of the road. Right next to the park bench.

"I need a break," Magnus said between pants. He was bent in half, his gloved hands on his knees and his back and thighs covered in snow and dirt. His hair was flattened to the back of his head and his cheeks rosy red from cold and exertion.

I couldn't take my eyes off him.

"There's a bench right here, old man," I teased him. "I'll wait while you catch your breath." I sat down on the freezing bench and patted the seat next to me.

We stayed long after he'd caught his breath. The seat was so cold, I soon couldn't feel my ass anymore, and I couldn't care less. My entire focus was on the boy next to me, on his stories, his smile. I wanted to stay there all night.

At one point, a guy in his thirties passed us slowly on his bike. Even on the zig-zags, only the most sporty ones manage the entire climb without stepping off the bike. We sat and watched him in silence until he disappeared over the hill.

I turned back to Magnus, expecting him to say we should get going to the party. Instead, he was much closer than before, his green eyes intense. "I really like you," he said. "Always thought you looked like a great girl and I'm happy to discover I was right."

I had no comeback. I stared wide-eyed at the sincerity of his expression, not quite able to comprehend he was saying this so seriously. My gaze dropped to his lips, which might be what got him moving.

Suddenly, his lips were on mine, one of his hands grabbing mine in my lap. We were both frozen but his breath was warm.

How could I have forgotten the memory of my sweetest kiss ever?

Well, not forgotten exactly. Hidden away in a colorful filing cabinet on a side aisle.

We never made it to the party. By the time we were too cold to stay there and keep kissing, it was almost two in the morning and we decided to turn our noses homeward instead. We walked slowly, holding hands, stopping frequently to kiss some more.

Maybe the fact it was a one-night thing is why I haven't thought back on it much. We didn't make any plans to meet up after we made it home. I guess it would have broken the magic of the moment. A couple of days later, Magnus went back to Oslo to study, and I continued being the girl nobody noticed.

And here I am again. A party on December 26th, slippery white roads, a slope to conquer. Except this time I'm alone and I'm going up instead of down. I've done at least eighty percent of the work already and I don't really need a break.

But it's the same bench.

My ass is frozen through. Trondheim by night is blinking up at me and a large catamaran is speeding away from the docks toward the mouth of the fjord. The faint sound of cars rises from the road down by the fort, but this area is empty and quiet. I'm supposed to be meeting my friends from high school and pretend we're eighteen again while drinking grownup drinks but I'd rather sit here and remember the boy who'd noticed me. Who thought I was special.

I keep saying I don't have many happy memories from high school. No miserable ones either, but I generally feel like I missed out on something intangible. Except maybe I didn't. I've just chosen not to think about any of it in years, good or bad.

I think I'll sit here and think about it now. A trip down the colorfully carpeted memory aisle. Enjoy the sparkling chandelier.

The squeaky crunch of someone walking on the frozen snow on the sidewalk breaks into my thoughts. Another lonely party-goer?

A lanky man with a beanie pulled down over his ears is trudging up the steep incline I climbed earlier. No zig-zags for this guy. He sees me sitting here and there's a hitch in his step.

He stops when he's on a level with my bench. Should I worry about being out here all alone in the middle of the night?

"I wondered if you might be invited to the same party. Home for the holidays, Emma?"

My jaw drops. I scramble to lean forward to get a better look at his face. "Magnus?"

Even surrounded by a trimmed blond beard and with the youthful roundness of his cheeks long gone, there's no mistaking the smile. It's too dark for me to make out the color of his eyes but I realize I don't need to—my memory remembers them perfectly.

"Was the climb too long for you? Getting lazy in your old age?"

I'm grinning from ear to ear. It's like my walk down memory lane took me back in time. Same place, same date, same weather, same guy. And yet it's different. I'm not the uncertain girl I was at eighteen. I've gained experience, lost innocence, learned about life.

And even through my adult lens, Magnus looks great. The boy he was back then, and the man he is now.

I plan to make a witty retort, show him I haven't lost my touch. Instead, I blurt out the truth. "I remembered our night here and stopped for a moment of nostalgia."

His smile softens. "Nostalgia is positive, right? So that's a good sign?" I scoot over on the bench and Magnus sits down, one elbow on the backrest as he faces me.

It never even occurs to me to hold back. We only knew each other for a night but it was enough for me to trust him not to hurt me if I'm honest. "That night was magical and holds nothing but positive memories for me."

"Oh, good. I was worried you might be mad I didn't try to keep in touch or anything."

I sit on my hands to keep from reaching out to touch him. Just because I've been reliving the memory of fifteen years ago doesn't mean he's in the same state of mind. "I could have reached out too. Maybe the memory was too perfect for a follow-up."

Magnus hums but I'm not sure it's in agreement. "I thought about reaching out. No, really! But I was in Oslo, you were here. We were just kids." He chuckles. "And you're probably right about not wanting to ruin a perfect memory."

"I'll have you know I'm always right." I lift my nose in the air.

"Sure you are. You were certainly right about us being able to slide down the hill without hiccups."

We burst out laughing.

As a comfortable silence settles, I sneak a glance at Magnus out of the corner of my eye. And am promptly busted because Magnus isn't pretending not to stare.

"What?" I say, my voice a little shaky. "Do I have something on my face?"

I can see the cheeky retorts lining up in his eyes. But he voices none of them. Just smiles at me.

"I found you on Facebook," he says. "Yeah, yeah, I know, very stalkerish. But from time to time something makes me think of Trondheim and I invariably end up thinking about you."

Wow, thinking about the city makes him go straight to me? I'm not sure if I should be worried or flattered. Maybe a little of both.

"So I looked you up. Saw you also live in Bergen and was *so* close to clicking that friend button."

My head whips around. "*Also?*"

His smile has a hint of uncertainty now. "I've been living in Bergen for five years. I work at the university."

I just sit there gaping. We've been living in the same city for five years? Somehow, even though I never thought about him, it feels like we missed out. We could have had so much fun.

Magnus clears his throat. "I think it's about time for me to point out I'm not here tonight because I'm stalking you. I'm honest to god invited to the same party. But I knew the friend who invited me is a friend of your friend, so..." His wince is kind of cute.

It's time I save him from the awkwardness. "I'm sorry I didn't stalk you back," I say with a smile. "I'm thinking maybe I should have."

I think about my friends. They're probably already drunkenly looking at pictures from our glory days and promising they'll meet up more often than once a year from now on. I'm sure it's loads of fun and I *do* want to meet my friends again. But I want to stay here even more, frozen ass and all.

"Will anyone miss you if you don't show up at that party tonight?" I ask.

Magnus cocks an eyebrow. "Are you asking me if my friends maybe won't notice if I'm not there? I am *not* invisible."

I take it as an invitation to give him a once-over. I take my time about it, too. "I know you're not." I nod toward the steep climb behind him. "But we never finished our descent. You up for a challenge? Or have you gotten scared in your old age?"

His smile lights up the cold winter night and his eyes sparkle like emeralds. "Now, look here, miss. I'm a Physics teacher and I'm telling you, there's no way we can slide down that entire slope in one go—or in one piece."

I bump my knee into his. "Nice upgrade. But I'm glad I'm not your student, because you are quite obviously wrong."

Magnus stands up, brushing off his pants and righting his beanie. He holds out a hand in invitation. "I guess I'll have to prove my theory. You game?"

Of course I'm game. Now the forgotten aisle of my memories has been reopened and the lights turned on in all the nooks and crannies, I'm not about to walk away and forget it again. I'm going to open wide the door from my boring adult main aisle so I won't lose my way. Maybe turn on some music, get a disco ball to go with the chandelier.

And I'm going to prepare a brand new filing cabinet for Magnus. It's going to be tall and green and have lots of little surprises that I can discover when I go exploring. I'll slip the files from that magical night all those years ago into the top drawer.

The memories we're about to make right now will go in the second one. I can already tell they're going to be awesome.

Author's Note

Thank you for reading *Down the Memory Aisle*. I hope you enjoyed it!

It turned out to be quite the trip down memory lane for me. Not because this story actually happened to me, but because the setting is the city in Norway where I grew up.

Trondheim in the snow really is magical.

I have a few more holiday short stories available, if you're interested. You can find them and a link to my website in the next pages.

And if you sign up for my newsletter, you can get the first Ghost Detective short story, *Just Desserts*, for free, in addition to being informed of all new releases.

I hope to see you around!

R.W. Wallace
www.rwwallace.com

About the Author

R.W. Wallace writes in most genres, though she tends to end up in mystery more often than not. Dead bodies keep popping up all over the place whenever she sits down in front of her keyboard.

The stories mostly take place in Norway or France; the country she was born in and the one that has been her home for two decades. Don't ask her why she writes in English—she won't have a sensible answer for you.

Her Ghost Detective short story series appears in *Pulphouse Magazine*, starting in issue #9.

You can find all her books, long and short, all genres, on rwwallace.com.

Also By R.W. Wallace

Mystery

Ghost Detective Novels

Beyond the Grave

Unveiling the Past

Beneath the Surface

Ghost Detective Shorts

Just Desserts

Lost Friends

Family Bonds

Common Ground

Till Death

Family History

Heritage

Ghost Detective Collections

Unfinished Business, Volume 1

The Tolosa Mystery Series

The Red Brick Haze

The Red Brick Cellars

The Red Brick Basilica

Mystery Collections

Deep Dark Secrets

A Thief in the Night

Time Travel (short stories)

Moneyline Secrets

Family Secrets

Romance
French Office Romance Series

Flirting in Plain Sight

Hiding in Plain Sight

Loving in Plain Sight

Holiday Short Stories

Morbier Impossible

A Second Chance

The Magic of Sharing

The Case of the Disappearing Gingerbread City

The Lucia Crown

Down the Memory Aisle

Young Adult Collections

Tales From the Trenches

Science Fiction (short stories)

The Vanguard

rwwallace.com/allbooks

www.ingramcontent.com/pod-product-compliance
Lightning Source LLC
LaVergne TN
LVHW041718060526
838201LV00043B/803